MAYLA RETURNS

DONNA DEAL

Printed in the United States of America

ISBN 978-1-958434-97-0 (sc)
ISBN 978-1-958434-98-7 (e)

Library of Congress Control Number: 2023910339

2023.06.23

MainSpring Books
5901 W. Century Blvd
Suite 750
Los Angeles, CA, US, 90045

www.mainspringbooks.com

Contents

Bringing Her Life to Normalcy

Annette, once the beautiful sex slave, Anna Bella, of her superior Toby Zobar from the Russian Federation Militia, has settled back to her own lifestyle with her family again and has concentrated solely on making a better, safer, and non-conflicting life for herself. Although she has been cautious through these years of raising her children, she has never forgotten how it was for her to be kidnapped and tortured for many years of her own life. She often is paranoid when she takes her children shopping or leaves them at a friend's house for an overnight stay. Her husband, Jim suffers vicious headaches and sometimes forgets who he is but be assured he never stops protecting his family and he too spends a lot of time lecturing and warning his children about the bad people in this world and what could happen to them at the blink of an eye. He is somewhat controlling of Annette, fearing that she may one day be taken away from him again.

Meantime, while Annette, Jim and the children have gotten their lives back together in the United States, things have escalated once again on the other side of their world. Even though there were bombs and gunfire that day during the escape of Annette (Anna Bella) and her friends from the Donetsk Airport, not everyone succumbed to their injuries that were involved in the militia. Survivors were taken to unknown areas and in time were healing from their major injuries. Some were crippled for life and were not able to return to their duties as soldiers. The pace is picking up again with the war and human trafficking continues to be a driving force for the Russian Federation. Plans are moving forward to bring a well-known stripper, along with her counterparts, back to the United States once again to recruit and introduce more young girls to dancing as strippers and provide entertainment to their sadistic comrades waiting in the underground. That's right, all of this is unknown to Annette and her family who are living their lives as normally as possible now and have become a very close net family with so much to offer their children for the future they have prepared for them.

Annettes friends Jan and Tina both have managed to stay in touch. Tina of course, spent some time in a federal penitentiary for a conspiracy conviction but was released on good behavior after 5 years. Both Annette and Jan have forgiven Tina because she risked her life as well and was the main reason, they made it home to their families after the devastating kidnapping.

Tina never had children and her husband at the time divorced her after she went to prison and most of her family lived elsewhere. Jan, however, was a single parent and her sixteen-year-old daughter, Trisha was about to graduate from high school along with Annettes daughter Mary, who is seventeen. It was to be an exciting commencement for both families and preparations were made for the after party with adult supervision. Annette and Jan were very strict on their daughters, so it was out of the question for them to go away after graduation like most teenagers are allowed to do.

It was a great celebration with family and friends afterwards and everyone seemed to have enjoyed the music and dancing as well as all the good food that was catered. Annette, Jim and Mary's brother, Mack, were so proud of Mary because she graduated as the valedictorian of her class. Jan's daughter too was honored as graduating in the top five. Both young girls were very smart and levelheaded and preparing for their future college education.

Summer Begins

Annette's daughter Mary is settling in to enjoy her summer before she makes her decision of which college she will attend since she has been accepted to three different ones. Jan's daughter Trisha wants to spend as much time with Mary as she can, since they both may be going their separate ways in the Fall. So much is happening for these two young women and their parents are so proud and excited for them. It's really time now for these ladies to watch their girl's grow into young women with so much energy and jest for life themselves.

Mary and Trisha were so into their education and making it to the top of their class, that having real teenage fun never crossed their minds. This is about to change as they sit down one night while watching a movie together and finally agree they really would like to take some modern dance classes together during the summer and make it fun to participate in events, demonstrating what they have learned together. Seems Mary had already talked to a dance instructor she met online, and the dance studio was only ten minutes from her house, so she and Trisha planned to go the next day to see what it was all about. They decided not to mention it to their parents right away as they wanted it to be a surprise. After all they had been told repeatedly that growing up and having some independence was part of what they were about to face in the real world.

As the two girls headed out the next morning to see what this adventure was all about, they laughed and giggled about how their moms were going to be shocked they were pursuing this on their own. They had arrived at the Beyond Beauty Dance Studio near the downtown mall and Trisha was a little nervous about going inside but Mary assured her that it was okay. Mary was already confident about what she wanted to do and having her best friend participate with her was exciting. Once inside the studio, the instructor greeted them with a smile and introduced herself as Miss Lilly. Both girls were amazed at how beautiful she was and what a glamours laid out studio with lots of exotic lights hanging from the ceiling and golden bars connected to the mirrored walls and beautiful marbled flooring. The class hadn't started, and they were the first to arrive, and Miss Lilly gave them a complete tour of the studio while waiting for the other students to arrive and for her to go over some parental permission forms with them since they both were under 18 years old. This was to be a class demo for them to just watch and take in all the different types of dances they would be learning to do.

Once the class was over, the girls decided to head home all excited about their experience and determined to join the dance group, but first they would need those permission slips signed!

This wasn't going to be easy, especially for Mary, as her mom, Annette, was very strict about meeting new people on her own without her knowing about it.

Breaking The News

It was Friday evening and Mary had asked her mom to invite Jan and Trisha over for pizza that night. Both girls planned to tell them about their plan and give them the permission forms to sign. Annette had already questioned Mary's absence that afternoon, which was making Mary very nervous because she had never lied to her mother before. Mary just simply replied that she and Trisha were on a mission and would talk to everyone about it at dinner. Her answer seemed to keep her mom calm yet anxious to find out what these two young ladies were up to.

The evening started off with everyone enjoying pizza and the parents having some wine. Mary's dad was out of town on a short business trip, so this was just all the females together.

Annette was busting at the seam to find out what these gals were up to, so she started by asking Mary to "spill the beans". Mary and Trisha nervously handed over the permission forms and information about the dance classes. Almost immediately Annette didn't want any parts of her daughter learning any kind of dance after everything she went through, it hit a nerve with her from years back of her kidnapping. She started questioning Mary about how she found this studio and how did she even come up with the idea of wanting to take dancing classes. When Mary replied that she came across this lady online, that totally flew up a red flag with Annette. Jan spoke up and basically agreed with Annette and told Trisha it was out of the question as well. Through the years these girls have been told about their moms' horrifying experiences and even though the two girls look at this as something to get involved for the summer, and like most teenagers, they don't see it as any danger to them. Both girls are now fighting back with their mothers on how they are being way overprotective, and they really want to do this. At this point both girls were told to go to Mary's room while their moms had time to go over the forms completely and discuss the matter. Once their moms were finished researching on the internet about this dance studio and the instructor, they called the girls to come downstairs. It was decided at this point for Annette and Jan to visit the dance studio themselves the next day to see what would be involved and for them to evaluate this entire situation. The girls immediately, like most teenagers, took offense, complaining that it would be embarrassing to them. Annette reminded them that someone had to pay for this, and she knew neither Mary nor Trisha would be able to afford it on their own. With that being said, the girls had no choice but to follow through with their moms' plans the next day.

Dance Studio Visit

The next morning after breakfast, Annette and Mary picked up Jan and Trisha and headed to the Beyond Beauty Dance Studio. Annette already jokingly addressing to Jan, "I wonder what the Beyond Beauty part of this business means?" Jan replied, "I guess we will find out in a few minutes", as they arrive at the studio. Both girls, still feeling embarrassed to have their moms make such an issue out of signing the permission forms, just kept quiet as they got out of the car.

Entering through the doors of this glamorously decorated studio, Annette and Jan immediately gasped for air. It was, again, bringing back memories of their experiences during their capture with Naughty Nata. The beautiful marble flooring, the gold bars, the mirrors were completely overwhelming at that very moment. Meantime, Miss Lilly, greets them with her open arms and speaks kindly to all of them as she starts to show

Annette and Jan around the studio and assures them of their safety policy and procedures to protect their daughters along with all the other students that come to her dance classes. Annette asked about the age groups of her students as she noticed some of her students already present appeared to be around Mary and Trisha's ages. Jan wants to collaborate on what types of dancing she is featuring in her classes and how this will be entertained to her daughter. Miss Lilly again, assures her that it is not exotic dancing if that is what she is worried about, we don't teach belly dancing here! Both girls giggle at that response and Annette orders them to be quiet.

Miss Lilly's personality seemed to be that of passion, dedication and professionalism, which did impress Annette and Jan. She continues to explain to the ladies that she teaches this age group to become successful dancers, they must have good balance, dexterity, and physical strength so they can move without losing their sense of rhythm. Her students are taught to let loose and express themselves to help the anxiety that a lot of teenagers go through at this age. Annette starts to relax and realize that her daughter could use some mobility lessons as Mary has always been a little clumsy and uncoordinated during her growing up process. Jan said it probably would help Trisha with her energy levels as she doesn't move around the house very fast.

By now the instructors are starting to come in for a pre-dance class meeting and Miss Lilly must excuse herself and told them to get with her receptionist to sign the paperwork and pay the twenty-five dollars a week fee per each girl for a period of 6 weeks which would take them through the summer. Annette and Jan decided they would allow the girls to join and participate in the studio's program but only if they were allowed to come in unannounced to check on them periodically. Miss Lilly agreed, if they didn't disrupt their sessions in any way. It was agreed upon and the paperwork got signed. The two girls just couldn't thank them enough for letting them do this. Mary at this point of the two girls, being the most excited!

As they left the studio, both Annette and Jan looked at each other with some apprehension about allowing their girls to participate but they were convinced it would be good for them. At this stage of their lives most girls are actively dating but Mary and Trisha had not shown an interest in boys. Allowing the girls to have dance as a hobby seemed like it would be going in the right direction. The girls would start almost immediately so they were excited to get home and prepare for the next day for their first session.

Obsession Sets In

Almost immediately, the girls become so into their dance routines, they forget to be aware of their surroundings going and coming to the dance studio. Obsession has taken them over and they are not interested in doing any other daily activities but were making sure they were on time for their classes. It's already been one month since they started, and Annette and Jan have only been to the studio one time to check on how the girls were doing. Apparently, they didn't feel the need to check up on them because at this point all they talked about was Miss Lilly and how she praised their dancing skills.

Mary was unaware of Miss Lilly's intentions and how she was so attentive to her especially and always asking her to demonstrate her dance routine to the newest students. Trisha noticed the special attention and felt Miss Lilly was becoming obsessed with Mary. She was not only jealous but a little suspicious.

Miss Lilly announced one night that she wanted two students to remain after class to help her put together a dance routine so they could get ready for an upcoming recital. She also invited one of her colleagues that was an instructor from another dance studio, to help. Turns out Mary was one of the students chosen but Trisha was not. This, of course, did not settle well with Trisha and that evening on the ride home with Mary, she told her how she felt and that she was concerned about Miss Lilly's obsession with Mary. Mary just laughed and told her she was just jealous that she didn't choose her. This didn't go well with Trisha, and she became upset and told Mary she thought she was going to quit the class. As Mary dropped Trisha off at her house, she told her to think about it and stop being so childish. Trisha slammed the car door and ran into her house.

Mary got home and entered the front door as usual, only to find her mother standing there waiting for her with cell phone in her hand. "Mary" she said, "what is going on between you two girls?" "I just got off the phone with Jan and she tells me Trisha came home very upset and told her that she did not want to go back to her dance classes?" Mary replies, "oh mom, she's just jealous because Miss Lilly wants me to stay after with another student to help prepare for the upcoming recital and she didn't ask Trisha". Annette follows up by saying that she doesn't want to see the girls fighting over this and tells Mary to make sure that Trisha gets picked up for the next class and they should talk to each other without being upset or jealous of one another. With that being said, the subject was dropped, and Mary went to her room to get ready for dinner but first she tried to call Trisha to ask her why she had to go straight to her mom about their business, but Trisha didn't answer the phone. She left her a voice mail message that she would not be able to pick her up and that she would have to drive herself to class the next day or get her mom to bring her because she was staying later that night to help Miss Lilly and the other instructor. She never heard back from her so Mary just went on to eat dinner with her parents and never discussed anything more about it with her mom. However, her dad had not been home much from traveling with his job, so he hadn't talked to Mary about how she was doing with her dance classes. Mary was always daddy's little girl so anything Mary did was okay in his book. After all, if you remember, poor Annette was Anna Bella for most of the child's life so it was evident that Jim would be the better parent who was always there for Mary. Sad but true that Mary just didn't understand where her mother was for all those years!

Mary tells her dad that she was hoping to be chosen as the dance Queen for the upcoming recital and he was so happy for her and gave her a big hug and congratulated her for doing a good job. Annette, on the other hand, reminded Mary that she had not completed her chores for the week, and it was time for her to get them done or she would not allow her to go to class the next day. Jim immediately told Annette not to be so hard on the girl, she will get them done. Mary decided to leave the table to go clean her room so she would not get punished.

The Next Day

Turns out that Mary did not pick up Trisha for class that day because she didn't hear back from her. When she got to the studio, she didn't see Trisha's vehicle, she just decided to go in thinking maybe her mom had already dropped her off. Miss Lilly greeted her at the entrance and told her that Trisha had called in sick and she was so sorry to hear that and asked Mary if Trisha had the flu. It was then that Mary told Miss Lilly the whole truth about Trisha's jealousness of her and said she probably would not come back. Miss Lilly told her how sorry she was that the two girls were not getting along but she would not get in between the two of them as she really liked both and wanted to see them get along.

Meanwhile, Miss Lilly introduced Mary to her colleague whom she referred to as Mayla. Mary was so excited to meet her and was happy that she was going to be helping with the preparations for the recital. Mayla took a real liking to Mary for reasons that were about to unfold and were unbeknown to Mary's mom. All in all, it was a great evening with the two instructors, but the other girl chosen never showed up for class or to help, so it was Mary all alone with them for the evening.

Miss Lilly was acting strange, and Mary just shrugged it off that she was preoccupied and busy going about her routine. However, Mayla on the other hand was there for an all-different reason other than what Mary was told about. She was more interested in finding out all she could about Mary, seemed like she wanted Mary to entertain her with her own routine she would be performing for the dance recital. They were in a part of the studio that Mary had never seen before. There seemed to be a secrecy about the room, but it was full of beautiful lighting and there was a different kind of interior decoration from the other part of the studio. The music was even different, an unrecognizable type from what Mary was used to dancing to. There was also a lot of smoke in the room like you would see on stage at a concert. Mayla explained to Mary that she was going to teach her how she could become the Queen of the recital by teaching her a different way to entertain her audience. Mary was very naive and absolutely had no idea what was about to happen. As Mayla was dancing around the room and demonstrating to Mary her style of dancing and her movements, Mary was enjoying a protein shake that Mayla had given her to drink earlier before they entered this special room. It was minutes into Mayla's dance that Mary started to feel very relaxed, and she too started dancing like Mayla. Before you knew it, they were dancing, laughing and Mary was moving her body in ways that she had never done before. She liked it and enjoyed her time with Mayla, her knew friend. Mary had no idea of what time it was, where she was, or even who she was. All she knew, she was having fun and enjoying the music. The protein shake she had consumed contained a memory suppression drug that was put in it along with ecstasy combined. She soon would not remember anything at all and only follow Mayla's instructions as she continued to dance more and more into the late evening. It's now past Mary's curfew of 10:00 pm and at this stage Mary doesn't even know where she is or is even the least bit concerned about it. She is being well coached by now and is feeling so into her own body movements.

Soon two men and Mayla are escorting Mary out to a dark colored SUV they had waiting for them. Miss Lilly has disappeared and can't be found by Mayla. Mayla could not be concerned at this point because her job was to get Mary out of the country which was why Mayla returned to the United States by commands of once again, Toby Zobar.

Thinking Miss Lilly must already be waiting in the SUV, Mayla confronts one of the soldiers to make sure everyone was in place, including Miss Lilly, and ready to get the hell out of there.

The soldier quickly responded by saying, "Miss Lilly would not be joining them." Mayla replies, "Where is she?". The soldier then informs Mayla that Miss Lilly met an unfortunate accident at the command of Toby. This was not an expected part of the plan, but Mayla knew how Toby operates and did not further question his horrific methods of getting rid of people. She too could be at risk if she failed to cooperate.

Where is Mary?

Annette was beginning to worry about Mary. It was 10:30 pm and her curfew was 10:00 pm and she had never been late before. When Mary didn't answer her cell phone, she decided to try Trisha's phone and when she answered she asked where the two of them were. Trisha immediately told her she had not gone to class today and told her the whole story about the day before and why she was so upset with Mary. She said that Mary had not been acting right and was becoming very close to Miss Lilly. In the meantime, Annette decides to tell Jim they needed to go to the dance studio to see if they can find Mary.

Approaching the parking lot, Annette and Jim don't see Mary's car and the studio is closed with no signs of anyone around. Annette begins to panic as it is now almost 11:00 pm and they haven't located their daughter. Jim drives around the entire building checking out any windows but the entire building was completely dark.

"Oh My God", cries Annette, after she calls Jan to see if by chance, did Mary come by there, "It's happening again", and Jan is trying to calm her down to find out exactly what she is talking about replies "What's happening Annette", Jan replies? After Annette explains what is going on, Jan rushes to talk to Trisha to see if Mary had been in touch with her all day. Annette calls the number on the paperwork to reach Miss Lilly, but the number is no longer available and there was no other way to reach her. She tried to email her and that too had been shut down.

It's soon realized in the midnight hour that because Mary and her car are missing, Jim decides to call 911 to report it and ask if there had been any accidents, describing their teenager's car and giving them a full description of Mary. He was told to stay where they were, and the police were on the way. Meantime, Jan, and Trisha show up on the scene and Trisha was crying saying she should have called Mary back and gone to class with her. When the police arrived, they soon discovered that the building was completely dark because the tenants had moved out unexpectedly and the entire Beyond Beauty Dance Studio was empty. The missing person investigation team arrives and begins taking fingerprints and looking for signs of a possible kidnapping. The only thing they found was an empty protein shake bottle, which they immediately sent to the lab for processing. Annette and Jan told their very own horrific kidnapping story to the police and even though it was too early on to put out a missing child alert, they decided not to wait, and an all-points bulletin was put out along with an amber alert. Description of Miss

Lilly was given by Annette and Jan to the police to further investigate her whereabouts.

Meanwhile, the investigation continues and the area around the dance studio has been secured and taped off for no one to enter the parking lot. The FBI has advised for Annette, Jim, Jan and Trisha to go home and wait to see if possibly they may get contacted for a ransom by the kidnappers. This was protocol in a situation like this and there would also be a search of Mary's bedroom, her computer and anything else they may find to be used for evidence to help the investigation. It was going to be a long and heart wrenching night for all involved.

Bringing in The FBI

It's been 6 hours since they discovered Mary missing and the FBI is now involved, and they are thoroughly questioning for more information from Annette and Jan about their very own kidnapping years ago that took them from America to Russian underground. Annette tells them she was taken and separated from Jan and was used as Toby Zobar's slave Anna Bella. He was possessed with her and was always a man to be feared of and always vowed that Anna Bella would never return to her country. She also told them he was killed the day they escaped the airport. With this information the police went immediately to Dallas International Airport to stop all international flights and have them searched by their agents. It was assumed that the kidnappers may be trying to use air transportation to get out of the country.

The FBI confirmed through Interpol that Toby Zobar did not die in the massive invasion at the airport that day. However, he spent months in the hospital and rehabilitation as the result of his injuries and now spends his time in a wheelchair still operating the militia with as much respect from his counterparts as he had when he initiated the capture of Annette and her friends that day. When Annette, Jim and Jan were told that he was still alive they immediately asked the FBI to talk with Tina who worked under him and had spent time in prison here in the United States for her part in the kidnapping, even though she was the very person that saved Annette's and Jan's life returning them to the United States. She knew Toby inside and out with all his schemes, motives, and plans to destroy anyone who got in his way.

Mayla's Orders

Mayla and the two soldiers from the militia that accompanied her with Mary, were hanging out in a mobile RV after they ditched the SUV, they used to kidnap Mary. This RV was parked in an abandoned mechanical garage a hundred miles away. The plan was to stay put and keep Mary sedated until they got word from Toby on how to proceed. During this period, the FBI had the airport still surrounded and continued to shut down all flights out of the country. Unbeknownst, of course to the FBI, Toby Zobar had other plans in the making and once he knew that Mary was coming around, he ordered Mayla to restrain her and make sure she interrogated her about her mother and father.

It wasn't long before Mary came too and didn't know what had happened or where she was. The only thing she knew was she was restrained and gagged so she couldn't talk. The two soldiers told her to corporate or her family would be killed. Tears are streaming down her face as she is scared for her life too.

Toby is now instructing the two soldiers to put into action his orders for getting out of the country but first he decides that now is the time to make his move to contact Annette, his long-lost Anna Bella, the Queen of his empire. He longed for her return to him, but also wanted revenge on her escape from him. He also wanted revenge on another previous member of his militia that turned against him. Tina was his next target, and he ordered his soldiers to make sure she was executed as soon as possible. After all she was the one who was able to maneuver the entire escape from Russia with his "Anna Bella" and Jan.

By now Mayla is planning for their escape out of the country once all of Toby's plans come together. Seems the FBI is unaware themselves of the alternative means of travel for this group of kidnappers. But first, she must make a surprise visit to Tina's home only to find that her house was surrounded by police presence, and she was unable to get near it. Seems the FBI already contemplated Toby's intentions and they now have Tina in a safe place to protect her. Tina once again may be able to take part in the investigation by helping to save Annette's daughter, Mary from this evil man.

The Letter

Prior to the kidnapping of Mary a landscaper, who was hired to clean up Annette's flower gardens was approached one day by one of Toby's soldiers disguising himself as a friend of the family, giving him a garden gnome that was a family heirloom and he wanted the family to be surprised so he asked if he would place it in her flower garden area close to the front entrance of Annette and Jim's home. The landscaper was asked to keep it a secret and offered a huge amount of money to say that it was part of his landscaping process to leave his customers a gift. With no further questions asked, the landscaper completed his work and so put the gnome in place.

Inside the garden gnome was the letter from Toby which was demanding ransom money of two million dollars for the return of Mary and that she, Annette, must be the one to make the hand off to a man disguised as a janitor at a nearby park facility. She must not bring anyone with her, be followed by someone or involve the police in any way. Toby has his own soldiers hard at work following and watching all the moves on Annette's home and they are certainly aware of the police presence in the area surrounding her home.

Toby, being the shrewd, manipulating, and dangerous man to all his peers would not hesitate one minute to killing Annette's husband and son execution style and it is forcefully put in his instructions to Annette in the letter.

Toby is ready to give Mayla the okay for Mary to call and talk to her mother, only. Mayla will have to make sure that it takes place where the number cannot be traced or tracked to a specific location. Mayla will keep Mary under her spell so she is not aware of her surroundings, and she will keep Mary tied up and subdued inside her human cage until Mayla can move forward with Toby's next step in his plan. Soon Mary is freed from the hooded mask she is wearing and becomes able to talk with Mayla by her side. She was told what to say and with a gun pointed directly to her head she must follow a written note that was placed in her hand to read to her mother. The call is made, and Mary cries out to her mom as Annette takes the call. "Mom, you must do what they say, or they will kill me. Please don't say anything and just listen. You must go to the gnome in the flower garden and retrieve a letter that was placed inside for you with instructions." The phone immediately goes silent as it is taken out of Mary's hands. By now Annette is panicking and of course she is surrounded by FBI agents along with Jim, Jan, and Trisha still by her side. The FBI was unable to trace where the call came from, and Annette runs outside to her flower garden and smashes it to the sidewalk to get the letter out of it. Annette is screaming to the top of her lungs as she now knows that Toby has her daughter and is now demanding a ransom for her return. The FBI took the letter and is reading it, evaluating its full content. They immediately scan it for fingerprints. Jim is telling the agents that he will not let Annette go without him, no matter what the letter states and he is furious, scared for his daughter's safety and ready to get his hands on Toby. After all he spent many years of suffering the loss of Annette to this man, thinking his wife was dead. One of the agents must calm him down and lay out on the table how this needs to be handled to find Mary's whereabouts and follow the kidnapper's orders to deliver the ransom money.

It's now really going to be another very long night and of course Jim will need to have a member of his financial department at his family-owned Texas oil company deliver the ransom money in cash to their home. He is not worried about anything but this dangerous attempt for Annette to get the money to the kidnappers without the thought of something happening to both she and Mary regardless. He knows how ruthless this Toby Zobar and his militia can be!! He wants justice but not at the expense of his daughter and wife.

CHAPTER 11

Tina's Plan of Action

Tina is more than willing to cooperate with the FBI on a plan that she herself has come up with to deliver the ransom money. She knows Toby will stop at nothing to get his hands on Annette and punish her in his own way, as well as use her daughter for sex trafficking in his own country just like he did his Anna Bella. He will stop at nothing to get the two of them out of the country and to torture them to the fullest. Tina's plan is to disguise herself as Annette and follow the ransom plan to the park. Annette doesn't want to take the chance, but she also knows that Tina is good at knowing how Toby operates and she finally agrees to the FBI to put it in place.

A rental vehicle has arrived in the driveway of Annette's and Jim's home and the person driving happens to be an FBI make-up artist that will help with disguising Tina as Annette. Tina already knows that it will have to be a perfect disguise to fool Toby and Mayla. Jim is relieved that Annette will not be the one to take the ransom. He's also amazed at how much Tina looks exactly like Annette when the make-up artist gets finished.

It's now time to leave and Annette is crying and praying at the same time for her daughter's safety. She wants Tina to be successful in delivering the money to the janitor in the park so they will release Mary. As Tina, disguised as Annette and wearing under her clothing a monitor, walks out of the house with a duffle bag full of money, she is being watched not only by the FBI but also by Toby's soldiers staged outside in the nearby woods on the ground with high tech binoculars ready to make a move on the vehicle as they get ready to follow it to the point of delivery. They too will be ready to fight off the FBI who may be secretly following her as well.

Toby has now been informed by his soldiers that Annette is on her way to the ransom location point and they are following her and so far, see no signs of her being followed by the FBI. However, they too are unaware of the drone that was released from the backside of the house as the car left the driveway and it's following high enough not to be seen by these soldiers.

As Tina reaches the park entrance, she follows, completely, Toby's instructions in his letter to park away from all other vehicles in an area that has been closed off which appears to look like a construction site. This way she can walk down the bike path near the waterfall area of the park where a man dressed in a park janitor uniform will be waiting to meet her.

Approaching the park janitor, Tina tries to give as much information about his description as she can whispering through her monitor even though a drone is in place in the air. Tina notices something is not right because the janitor seems to be preoccupied with a woman walking a dog. The closer she gets to the janitor she can hear him telling the woman that she must turn around and walk her dog in the opposite direction. The woman appears to be arguing with him aggressively that she must go in the same direction to get to her vehicle parked nearby. She is very persistent with the janitor to get out her way. This seems to frustrate the janitor and he pushes the woman to the ground and the dog attacks him violently. Tina takes this opportunity to inform the FBI of what is happening, unbeknown that the drone is in the air above her. Next thing she knew, there were two men grabbing her and taking the duffle bag from her hands and dragging her back to the construction site. By the time they reach it, there too was FBI agents surrounding the entire park and waiting to take these two men and the janitor into custody. Seems the lady with the dog was also an undercover FBI agent and she was monitoring the phone being used by the janitor who was in touch with Mayla and now the FBI had the location of where Mary was taken.

Approaching The Kidnapping Site

By now there are many agencies involved in this kidnapping to include Immigration and Customs Enforcement (ICE) Homeland Security Investigations (HSI) Federal Bureau of Investigations/FBI Child Exploitation and Human Trafficking Task Forces along with Special Weapons and Tactics (SWAT)…

They are all gathered and ready to take on this situation beyond the capabilities of local law enforcement, surrounding this abandoned mechanical garage on the outskirts of Dallas, Texas. There is no room for mistakes for these terrorist soldiers and their leader to escape the United States. Toby Zobar is in hiding here in the states while giving orders to Mayla and his men. They all must be captured and the safe return of Mary to her parents and family.

As these brave men and women enter the building to take over these soldiers and counterparts, they focus clearly on saving Mary. The building is dark with signs of human life inside the building. They can hear whom they think are soldiers talking and a woman ordering them to get Mary ready for transporting to leave the country. One of the soldiers decided he wanted to have some fun with "Virgin" Mary as he called her before they began their journey home. He approaches the cage that Mary has been living in since her capture, opens the door and proceeds to grab her forcibly but like her mother, she's a fighter and she spits in his face, thrashes her feet at his private parts and vows he will never have her. He throws her to the cold and dirty floor and proceeds to rape her only at that very moment he hears the sounds of gun fire, and he runs to see what is happening leaving the cage open for Mary to escape. Mayla catches her and leads her to the back entrance of the building and proceeds to get away with her. Mayla was a strong woman but now that Mary has escaped from the cage, there was nothing to hold her back. She swings at Mayla with an iron pipe she grabbed at the door and knocks Mayla off her feet. Mary runs out the door screaming into the arms of several FBI agents. Thanks to Mary's quick thinking, Mayla has now been captured, along with the soldiers of the militia and now they all will face the consequences of their actions with imprisonment for life in our country, the United States of America. Toby Zobar was captured on a train just outside the border to Canada, disguised as a priest in a wheelchair on a flight scheduled to leave for Russia.

It's time to put an end to this horrifying experience for Annette (Anna Bella) Jan, and Tina, the surviving victims of sex trafficking from the days of *Naughty Nata and Anna Bella*. Mary is safe, unharmed sexually, but it will take time for her to heal of all she has been through during this kidnapping experience.

Human Trafficking Prevention
Month/Homeland Security

Every year since 2010, the President has designated January as National Human Trafficking Prevention Month. Since that time, the month has become a time to raise awareness about how we all can prevent this crime by learning how to identify and report human trafficking.

Resource Information provided by https://www.dhs.gov and go to topics for Human Trafficking.

Visit https://www. state.gov/20-ways-you-can-help-fight-human-trafficking/

www.ingramcontent.com/pod-product-compliance
Lightning Source LLC
Chambersburg PA
CBHW061501210726
48287CB00007B/2612